The Wand Chronicles

Book 0: The Prequel

Michael Ross

This book cover and illustrations were lovingly

designed and produced by Magdalena Adić.

(xdmaggy@gmail.com)

The Wand Chronicles – The Prequel

The Wand Chronicles – The Prequel

ᴗᴗᏕᖵᎭ꞉�II�Ꮢᴗ ᴕᏕ꞊ᏕᏕᎤ꞉IIᏕᎭI꞉ᴗ ᏕᖴᏢ ᏕᏕ ᏕᴕᴗᏒᴕᏒᏒᎭᎮᎮ꞉II ᴗᏒᴕᴕ꞉ᴗᴗ

Once you open yourself up to change,

you will begin to live, learn and evolve.

ᴗᴗᏕᴕᎭ꞉ᴗᴗᏒᴕ ᴕᏕᏕᏕ ᏕᎭᏒᴕᴕᴕ ᴕᏒᴕᴗᏒᴕIᴗ꞉II ᴗᏒᴕᴕᴕ ᴗ꞉IIᴗᏕᏕᴕ ᴕᴗᴕᴗᏒ꞉II

All quotes and any image, all extracts from book 1, 2 & 3
at the beginning of each chapter, including the Prologue and Epilogue
and the whole of the contents are copyrighted © 2019
to Michael Ross and Magdalena Adić.
All rights reserved. No part of this book may be used or
reproduced in any manner whatsoever including internet
usage, without written permission from the Author.

ISBN: 9781687002396

The Wand Chronicles – The Prequel

A Note from the Author:

You will notice at the start of the prologue and the two following chapters, an elvish script.

This is no ordinary elvish script, it could not be described as 'high' elvish. It is in fact the elvish dialect that is only spoken on Laniakeea.

It is called 'Solderran'.

Elvish is usually written in purple on Laniakeea, this color is extracted from the leaves of the Melroon tree.

To the Laniakeeans, the color purple is associated with all things magical.

Immediately following the elvish, is the translation into English.

These sayings are deeply rooted in every aspect of the Laniakeean way of life.

Our own word, 'affirmation', loosely comes from the Laniakeean word, 'Palnath'an', or ⸘ᄼᏞᏦᏞᎧᏞᎧᏞᏞ

One of the most well-known sayings on Laniakeea is –

'ᏞᏞᎧ ᏎᏵᏰᎧᏞᏵ ᏒᏔᎧ ᏎᏵᏦᎧᏞᏞ ᏔᏦᎧᏦᏞᏦᏵᏔᏞᏔᏔᏔᏦᏦᏞᏵᏞ ᏎᏵᏦ ᏦᏞᏦᎧᏞᏞ'

Which translates as –

'If you say it, you'll believe it. If you believe it, then you'll do it'

The Wand Chronicles – The Prequel

CONTENTS

IMAGES:

P.T.O.

DEDICATIONS

I dedicate this book to my sons, Aidan, Ben and Oliver and to my Brother Kevin.

To my amazing Beta readers Emma Healey.

To my editor, Philip Newey of All-read-E :
http://philipnewey.com/All-read-E.htm

To my illustrator, Magdalena Adić

To Alan J. Hesse, for his invaluable climate change facts:
(The Adventure of Polo the Bear: a story of climate change)

About the Author:

Michael has written a comedy, (Memoirs from the S.B.C.) a true-life story, (Just Five more Minutes) for which he won the Independent Audiobook Awards 2019. And has now embarked on an epic fantasy trilogy. This prequel will set the scene for the Wand Chronicles trilogy, which is an amalgamation of his creative ideas, thoughts and experiences. Essentially, he is writing these books for himself, but he genuinely hopes you will enjoy them as well.

Post-apocalyptic Earth. 2087.

(In the city that was once known as Stockport)

PROLOGUE

ᔑᓭ╎リ⣌⊣ᒷリ ᔑᒲᔑ⣌リ ᒷᓭᔑᒷᔑ ⣊⣏⨅ᔑᓭᒷᓭ ⣊⣊ᒷᔑᒷᔑ⣌リ╎リ⣌ᒷᔑ

(We all make mistakes. We need mistakes in our lives.
How else would we learn?)

If we were eternal beings and had seen the planet Earth in all its glory when it formed, we would have been impressed. As time marched onwards, the evolution of the diverse plants and animals would have taken our breath away.

We would notice a living, breathing sentient being emerging, called a human being, and would think this planet Earth would be a jewel in the cosmos.

How wrong we would be. How could these intelligent beings wreak such devastation on such a beautiful planet, which was, of course, their home! By the beginning of the year 2087, there had been three major world wars, with all the suffering and loss of life these brought with them, and it would not stop there. There would be the devastation caused by human-induced climate change, experienced as abnormal weather patterns, melting polar ice caps, and coastal regions disappearing underwater.

A double whammy of destruction. Enough to make visiting beings from another galaxy or parallel dimension openly weep.

And the visiting beings would question the motives of the human beings that had committed such irresponsible acts of wanton destruction.

But we know why, don't we?

Power struggles, politics, greed, money, religious diversity, short term visions: all would contribute to the sad and sorry state the Earth was in.

Life, as we know it on our planet, was ailing. The planet had sustained all sorts of life for millions of years, and it was being thanked for that lifegiving energy by humans committing selfish acts of mindless destruction. By now there was a turning tide of responsibility, an awakening, and a global positivity that wanted to act to save the planet.

Was it too late to turn back this tide of destruction?

Well, the short answer is: perhaps not.

Humans are both the problem and the solution. It is a shame not all humans think alike; it is the 'true children of the Earth' that plant the seed for global change. It required a little help, and so there were other more powerful forces at work that had given humans the time to put their affairs in order, willing them to turn back from the brink of annihilation. They had now decided that enough was enough. They would step in and help save the planet.

The most powerful of those entities was the sentient lifeforce known as the Chrandalis Initiation. And what made the Chrandalis Initiation want to intervene?

It was the genuine passion of a Swedish schoolgirl who described herself as a climate-change warrior. In her own words, she wanted to save the world by changing the rules.

The Chrandalis Initiation was impressed that it took the determined courage of this Swedish schoolgirl to make all the adults and politicians worldwide sit up and listen. To point out that it was intolerable to ignore the signs of our planet's abuse. It was our home. And it needed to be saved. *NOW!*

The Chrandalis Initiation is a collection of sentient beings, older than time itself. They were responsible for creating vast dimensions and a multitude of cosmii.

Earth belonged to one such arrangement of planets, in a particular dimension that was shared by other species of sentient beings, all at differing stages of physical and spiritual evolution.

The humans on earth were very young as a species. It was just over three million years since the first ape appeared.

For the Chrandalis Initiation to intervene, they needed to find another, much more advanced species to act as their catalyst to improve and help the planet Earth. As it happened, in a parallel dimension within the same cosmos were the elves of Laniakeea. Laniakeea, in English, is the 'Immeasurable Dimension.'

The Chrandalis Initiation was delighted because, unbeknownst to the developing humans, the elves had been studying the human's way of life since they first appeared. It was a one-way affair, of course. It had to be that way. To not interfere in the development of a new species was paramount. And that was how it was always going to be. But since the Chrandalis Initiation were the rule makers, they decided to allow the elves to make physical contact with the humans.

The Chrandalis Initiation would not do so themselves, but used some special spiritual beings they could call on to mastermind the whole process; in this case, to introduce a highly evolved species of elf for the purposes of improving the situation the humans were now facing.

They brought in a species of Traveler, who, in the background, out of sight, would initiate a series of events in which the Elves and humans would naturally come together.

The particular Traveler given this task was Andropalathan the 118th. As you delve into the Wand Chronicles, you will meet this Traveler in much more detail. You will realize how powerful he is, and how he is able to manipulate events to a successful conclusion.

But even the best-laid plans can go awry. The manipulative journey of the Traveler will encounter cracks, landslides and events beyond even his control on the road to success.

For now, let us investigate exactly where the humans were in the beginning of the year 2087, what they were doing and who the main players would be.

Similarly, let's be a 'fly-on-the-wall' of the elves of Laniakeea, determine how much more advanced they are than the humans, their similarities (and there will be many) and differences.

The Wand Chronicles – The Prequel

Let's prepare ourselves for the tumultuous change of fortunes that was to come on 30 June, 2087, which would affect the lives of the Elves, humans, and, consequently, many more species, not only within our dimension and cosmos, but many others as well.

Welcome to The Wand Chronicles

The Wand Chronicles – The Prequel

Brough Manor situated in the United European
Landmass, England States.

(Designed and built by the French Architect, Pierre-Louis
Moreau-Desproux in 1731)

CHAPTER 1

The Earthan Dimension

ᔕᖆᐢᐟᑌᐢᕑ᠁ᐣ ᕑᢣᐠᐁ᠑ ᕽᢣᖆᐣᐟᐢᐟ ᐁᕑ ᕑ᠑ᖆᐠᐢᐟ᠁ᐣ ᕑᔕᖆᐠᐤᕑ ᕑᢣᐠᐁ᠑ ᖆᐠᕑᕽᕽᕽᔕᕑᕑᔕᖆᐠᕑ
(Ask your hearts, not your head, if you want an honest answer)

There was no doubt about it. Brough Manor was a spectacular family home. It had been in the Brough family for over three hundred years. It was vast, with two libraries, two kitchens, eleven bedrooms, nine of which were en suite, two study rooms and so on.

Externally, there were staff cottages and large stables, housing over thirty-five horses, including a collection of beautiful pure-bred palominos.

All this set in four hundred and sixty acres, in which there was a large forest. On one edge of the forest was a smaller wood called "Wimberry Wood," named after the prolific number of wimberry bushes which produced the small purplish berries regularly picked to make jam and, in particular, the much sought after wimberry pies. It was also home to large families of wild boar.

After the ravages of three world wars and climate change, Earth was very different from what it had been less than eighty years ago. By 2080, fossil fuels were depleted. Fuel as such was non-existent, unless for absolute emergencies. Landmasses were quickly submerging under the rising water levels due to melting polar ice caps. The population of Earth that remained had reverted to harnessing wind power for transport, or using horses, as Brough Manor was doing. Research into solar technology for energy was a priority. Batteries had become much more advanced. They were smaller and could hold more charge, therefore lasting so much longer. Electric trucks and cars were being developed.

If we could step into a time machine to take us forward eighty years, what is the first thing we would notice from outer space, looking back on planet Earth?

We would notice Greenland was now in fact green! The ice had melted, and the world's largest island had become a haven for the migration of people from all over the world. There was a civilized infrastructure, schools, hospitals, businesses and so on. A branch of the United European Landmasses was now on

Greenland, coordinating their efforts to bring about positive changes.

In other areas of the planet there were continuing advancements in technology, with the treatment of common medical problems in "medicenters" using a remarkable machine that could diagnose and treat most medical issues, even those that at one time would have required surgery or invasive treatments, such as cancer. There was a piece of technology called the "Headcomm" or HC, a small black button implanted behind the right ear of every human now alive. It was a combination of a laptop and a mobile phone.

It was mandatory to implant these HCs into every newborn baby. It held all records of the person wearing it, including internet banking accounts, job skills, and messaging services, but it also told the government who you were and where you were. Attempts to remove it resulted in immediate death. Once implanted, it was there to stay.

Consequently, crime was dramatically reduced, disabilities eradicated, specific skills assessed, so humans were placed in the right industry.

As a consequence of the landmasses disappearing underwater, new re-named land masses were being colonized.

There were no more "countries" as they were once known. Different races and cultures and languages were merging.

Importantly, humans finally recognized the mistakes they had made and wanted to put it all behind them and make the Earth a better place in which to live. There was generally a positive feel to it all.

But no matter how positive the consensus was, there would always be the "bad" apple in a barrel of good ones; such is the nature of the Human Being.

It is now the 28 June, 2087. The "Squire," if you like, of Brough Manor was Lord Arlo Brough. A massive, overweight brute of a man, who waddled rather than walked, whose red hair was beginning to show flashes of white. It was shoulder length, and, although he was balding slightly on his crown, he scraped it into a top knot on his head.

Lord Brough was head of the UEL, the United European Landmass. He was also a senior judge, officiating over domestic affairs within the UEL. He was married to Lady Romiley Brough and he had two sons, Hugo and Kayon, both in their early twenties, and a daughter, Helena, who was just twenty. He did have another son, a mixed-race boy called Maxx, after an illicit affair with a cleaning lady of West Indian origin, who worked within Brough Manor. She disappeared under very suspicious circumstances several years ago, and, although officially he had had to admit that he was the father of Maxx, under no circumstances was Maxx going to get any share of his lands and properties, which should have rightly been allocated to him.

Arlo Brough didn't have an ounce of compassion. This was illustrated in the judicial cases he presided over. He readily handed out extensive prison sentences when they only warranted a slap on the wrist or a severe warning. He was hated and despised everywhere.

His eldest son, on the other hand, was the epitome of decency and fairness. At just twenty-three, he was already a military general and head of security for the UEL. He was also very handsome, with a mass of dark curly hair, and a curious scar down one side of his face. This, together with his confident nature, seemed to be a magnet for all the available women in the area. However, the head of the stables, Charlie Andover, a red-headed, vivacious woman of thirty-two, had already enticed Hugo, at the tender age of eighteen, to relinquish his virginity in the hay barn behind the stables one hot and passionate humid evening.

There would always be an unspoken attraction between them, but, such was the confidence and playful nature of Charlie

Andover, whenever their paths met she would tease and taunt Hugo mercilessly. Even now, when he was in the lofty position of general and head of security, Charlie could still make him squirm and wish he was somewhere else.

Hugo was not ready to settle down. He was ambitious, but not to the detriment of others. He preferred to spend his leisure time pursuing sporting activities.

His aide, both militarily and in private life, was a Chinese man called Ding Ling. "Dingy" to those close to him. Hugo had rescued him from a cruel uncle, who used to beat him mercilessly, on one of his campaigns in the South China regions. Ding Ling was quite small. He was extremely brave. He had a gentle sense of humor, and was always ready to bring into a conversation one of Confucius's many sayings. For example, Ding Ling was advising Hugo that he should only work on one problem at a time. To illustrate this, he would say, a little too loudly, "Confucius would say, do not swallow sleeping tablet, if you have already swallowed a laxative pill."

Hugo was in the large county kitchen at Brough Manor with Ding Ling. They were both sneakily trying to pinch some of the hot, freshly baked scones that the head chef, Jemima, had just taken out of the oven.

Jemima had, of course, spotted what they were up to and, with a wry smile, she shouted at them both, "Now clear off, you two. Those are for some guests that are arriving any time now. It's a good job I made a few extra. I had a feeling there were some scone thieves close by." She put her hands on her hips and laughed out loud.

Hugo and Ding Ling tiptoed out of the kitchen into an anteroom to finish off the scones with some of the homemade strawberry jam and clotted cream.

Ding Ling turned to Hugo and said, "Master, cook a very large lady, isn't she?"

"Well yes, Dingy," said Hugo, "She is, but don't forget that universal saying: 'Never trust a skinny cook.' You have to admit her cooking is impressive, and she even prepares Chinese delicacies just for you."

As they sat and ate the hot scones, they were discussing and planning the wild boar tagging hunt that was to take place in Winberry Wood in a couple of days' time.

Ding Ling said to Hugo, "So who is accompanying you on this hunt, Master?"

"Well," said Hugo, "I think you know them? Jeremy, my second-in-command at security at the UEL, and Gavin, a friend who was in the same intake to military officer training at Sandhurst as me."

"Ah yes, Master, I know them well. I will make sure your stallion, Firemaker, is prepared, and also horses for Jeremy and Gavin. Will also ensure the beaters are positioned at the northeast corner of Winberry Wood to push the boar down towards you. What time you want to begin, Master?"

"Hmm. There lies a small problem, in that I will be in a security meeting until early evening, so envisage being in Winberry Wood at around 7:30 p.m. The problem is, by the time the beaters start working their way down, the light will be fading, so as the boar reach us, we will probably only have about an hour of decent light left. Anyway, there should be just enough time." Hugo began to smile. "Why don't you join us, Dingy?"

"Master," said Ding Ling, "as you know, me very brave Chinaman, but some things scare my pants off. Fast, bristly pig animal, with tusks, running at you, at hundred miles an hour, with no anger management skills, not my cup of china tea!"

Hugo laughed, and so did Ding Ling, whose face creased up. Even his laughter was infectious. He always sounded a little like a chipmunk when he laughed.

When they had finished their scones, they got down to the serious side of planning the wild boar hunt. This was one of Hugo's favorite pastimes. He would insist on using only a retro gun, challenging to use when standing still, never mind on a galloping horse that was weaving in and out of the trees. Of course, it was a certified "hunt," and the boars would not be killed, only tagged for scientific purposes.

On odd occasions the boar population would spiral out of control, and there would be a culling operation. The rules of culling were stringent. Only a specific number of boar would be dispatched; usually those that were old or sick, and the manner in which they were killed would be as humane as possible.

The excitement in Hugo was already building. It was all to do with how many boar the individual team members could tag. On more than one occasion Hugo's father, Lord Arlo Brough, had wanted to be a part of the team, but the moment he stated he would bring a shotgun with live ammunition to, using his words, "blast the little beggars into smithereens," Hugo flatly refused to have him along. In this case, the law was on Hugo's side.

No human or boar would be hurt. For Hugo it would always only be about the excitement of the chase.

The Wand Chronicles – The Prequel

Laniakeea

(Translates as the 'Immeasurable Dimension'. This elvish
dimension contains the most powerful wand in the cosmos,
called Elvina)

CHAPTER 2

The Elvish Dimension of Laniakeea

ᚾᛁᚾᚷᛁᚾᛋ ᛏᚾᛁᚾ ᛏᛋᚵᚵᛋᛗᚢᛁᚾ ᚴᚱᛏᚾ ᛏᛋᚵᚵᛋᛗᚢᛁᚾ ᚱᛋ ᛏᚾᛑᚢᛏ ᚱᛏᛑᚴ

(There is no greater feeling than performing an act of random kindness)

Laniakeea is a parallel dimension, running side by side with the planet Earth and its solar system. If we compare the emergence of humans some three million years ago to that of the elves of Laniakeea, who have been around for nearly six and a half million years, you can imagine that the process of evolution has resulted in beings far more advanced than humans.

And this is, in fact, the case. Before we explore the differences, it is worth noting that there are many similarities. We both have arms, legs, a torso, a head, two eyes and two ears, and are approximately the same height. Both species walk upright. They have similar emotions, including humor, anger, and so on.

Even on Laniakeea, long before the elves were introduced, the Chrandalis Initiation had created a sentient, tree-like being called the Sola Tree. After millions of years, these Sola Trees could also create simpler dimensions, and so it was that a Sola Tree created the dimension of Laniakeea. There were, by now, a number of Sola Trees creating other dimensions, and there was a ruling body called The Sola Continuum, a collection of six of the wisest Sola Trees. It would "police," for want of a better word, the evolutionary paths of sentient beings introduced into newly formed dimensions, all under the watchful eye of the Chrandalis Initiation.

Let's explore the Laniakeean elves in particular.

Generally, they are around seven feet tall. The same body shape as humans, but with spindlier arms and legs. They are completely hairless, except for the hair on their heads, which becomes their crowning glory. Typically, blonde or white blonde, there are a few darker, more colorful variations. They have an elvish dialect called Solderran, but communicate telepathically most of the time.

Their brain is fifteen per cent larger than the average human brain, to accommodate telepathy, but also so that they can perform basic magical skills. But it doesn't stop there. Humans can only use up to thirty per cent of their brain at any one time, but the elves may use up to ninety-five per cent. To help with this, elves have two hearts, a larger one in the middle of the chest that pumps blood around their body, and a slightly smaller heart, situated in the upper left cavity of their chest. This works independently of their main heart and is used solely to oxygenate their brain to keep it functioning at full capacity.

The blood of an elf is very bright red in color, illustrating how highly oxygenated it is. The advantage is that elves can run faster, for longer, before needing to rest.

The lifespan of an elf is approximately two hundred and fifty years. With advances in genetics and medicine, this is increasing all the time.

There are, of course, exceptions to this rule. During the formation of this dimension, the Sola Continuum decreed that there should be an elf Queen, who they named Queen Haruntha. They gave her the capacity to reincarnate. Quite beautiful and accomplished, Haruntha is loved by all her subjects.

But there is another elf—and I use that term loosely—who reincarnates called Elfistra. Elfistra is a sorceress, and again was commissioned by the Sola Continuum. Her purpose is twofold: protection of Laniakeea and its Elves, and security of the cosmos's most powerful wand, called Elvina. Elfistra doesn't look like an elf. Her body is covered in thousands of small silver and black scales. She has long black hair and vivid red eyes. When she is upset or angry, all the scales rise to reveal angry red skin underneath.

Her magical abilities are limitless. When these inherent powers are combined with the powerful effects of Elvina the wand, this makes her one of the most powerful sorceresses, not only in this dimension, but many others as well.

There is also her aide, Mandaz. He is also magical and reincarnates, but is deformed, with one large eye beside a much smaller one. He has withered, deformed legs that he has to drag behind himself, and his hands and feet are large and ungainly. His skin is composed of millions of small pustules that are continually popping, so a slimy yellow discharge covers the large lump on his right shoulder and constantly drips onto the floor. He has a magical staff called the Tazareth that he uses to help move around. He also exudes a constant aroma similar to that of rotten meat. He is a great supporter of Elfistra and Laniakeea.

Describing Elvina as the most powerful wand in the cosmos doesn't do her justice. When on her own, not a lot happens. It is only when she integrates with a chosen elf that her power becomes available. The process of Elvina's integration with Elfistra has to be seen to be believed. Elvina, when at rest, is kept in an ancient magical box, called the Spiriten, covered in magical incantations and inlaid with precious stones. Inside the box, Elvina is laid onto lush, purple crushed velvet. If you observe her carefully, she appears to breathe. The main body of Elvina is ancient carved Sola Tree wood, but at the top is a globe filled with swirling gold and green mists, containing constructs from many alien dimensions.

A handful of elves on Laniakeea are termed "Elfanda," which translates as "special one." They have above-average magical abilities. One such Elf is Allana Yana-Ash. She could also integrate with Elvina.

No one else can usually do this. In fact, it would be destructive to any ordinary Elf. However, it is written in the prophecies that there will come a time when an "ordinary" Elf, or even one of a different species, will need to be able to integrate with Elvina. It is written that this person or species will have a heart or hearts that are true, honest and compassionate.

Because of the enormous power of Elvina, there have been many attempts over the previous six and a half million years to steal her. So far none have succeeded. A few times thieves have managed to smuggle her out of Laniakeea, but somehow, in the end, she has been returned to her rightful place.

Her rightful place is not just in her Spiriten box, which is powerful in its own right, able to become invisible when the need arises. When at rest this box is kept within the Sola Tree on Laniakeea.

In the depths of the Sola Tree, beyond its roots, is a magical maze, in the center of which is a golden and intricate box, in which the Spiriten containing Elvina is kept.

It is worth noting, if you are human and reading this, that Laniakeea is vast. If you were to place a period or full stop on a map of Laniakeea, that full stop or period would represent the size of planet Earth!

Let's explore some of the other differences between a human and an elf, but, before we do, how can we explain the similarities? At the beginning of the formation of the cosmos by the Chrandalis Initiation, the Sola Continuum was given some precious DNA strands of a species that existed even before the Chrandalis Initiation became who they are. The Sola Continuum was instructed that whenever they formed a new dimension within a cosmos, they were to seed that dimension with some of these precious DNA strings. The Sola Continuum was able to alter the DNA, but only very slightly, leaving it to evolution to determine how these new species would form and ultimately expand. Hence the similarities between the elves and humans.

Considering the elves have been in existence for almost three and a half million years more than humans, evolution has created some significant differences. The female elf has lost the ability to produce elf offspring; in fact, it is the male elf that is now able to produce new offspring. The male elf is now hermaphroditic. They can self-fertilize.

A typical elf family unit on Laniakeea is comprised of a male and two females. The males do not form any kind of sexual relationship with a female. That is left to the leading elf female, who will develop a relationship with another female elf, and that elf will be invited to create a family unit. All three would be responsible for the care, love and upbringing of a young elf. There are many other minor differences between humans and Elves that will become apparent when reading the Wand Chronicles trilogy.

Once humans became a little more—for want of a better word—"civilized." A secret portal was created between Earth and Laniakeea. Elf explorers, mainly the elf equivalent of scientists, were able, in disguise, to integrate into human communities to investigate all aspects of human life. They were under strict instructions never to interfere with the evolutionary progress of humans and were there purely as observers. One such scientist was the Elfanda, Allana Yana-Ash, who was mentioned previously. Allana was a scientist concerned with communication and language and would gather information, then pass it on to other interested Laniakeeans in their equivalent of universities.

The prophecies stated that a time would come when the humans and elves may need to integrate, so these observations were part of the preparations for that time, if indeed it came to be.

Generally, Laniakeeans were very honest. Wars did not exist. Preserving the physical and spiritual aspects of their dimension was paramount. The greed, anger, wars, and the irresponsibility with which humans treated their planet greatly saddened the Elves. They understood, because they had been in a similar circumstance in the early stages of their evolutionary development, but the beauty of evolution had ironed out the destructive elements.

The elves questioned how far the humans would travel down this destructive path before something radical happened to make them more aware of the need to treat their planet and each other with more love, care and attention. It was reaching a point, according to the elves, of no return. They could envisage a time very soon when the humans would destroy themselves and their planet, and this was very disturbing to the elves.

But they could do nothing and were not permitted to interfere. All they could do was watch as the beginning of the end seemed to be approaching.

It became so serious that the Sola Continuum decreed that the secret portal to planet Earth be closed to the Laniakeean scientists. This happened in the Earth year 2086.

The Wand Chronicles – The Prequel

The Sola Continuum met with the Chrandalis Initiation to decide what they could do to save the humans and their planet. Something desperately needed to be done, and sooner rather than later, so they issued an invitation to the Traveler, Andropalathan the 118th, to attend the source of the Chrandalis Initiation. The Sola Continuum would also be in attendance, and they would formulate a positive plan of action to save Earth and the humans.

Following are extracts from:

Book 1: Elfistra the Sorceress

Book 2: Kia the Empath

Book 3: Eternity

(Please read the Author notes page number 59)

Elfistra the Sorceress when she has fully integrated with the most powerful wand in the cosmos, Elvina.

AN EXTRACT FROM BOOK 1:
ELFISTRA THE SORCERESS

꘡꘡꘡ ꘡꘡꘡ ꘡꘡꘡ ꘡꘡꘡ ꘡꘡꘡ ꘡꘡꘡ ꘡꘡ ꘡꘡꘡ ꘡꘡꘡

(Challenges are there for a reason. To learn. To live. To love)

General Hugo Brough sat on Firemaker, his favorite stallion, listening intently to the beaters drumming and shouting behind him in the forest.

Dressed in brown military leathers, he was a handsome man, tanned, with a short beard and a curious scar running down his cheekbone from the side of his left eye. A retro gun was strapped to his back. He preferred it because it was very basic and needed much-developed skill to wield effectively, giving an animal a fairer chance to escape.

At only twenty-three years of age, he was a force to be reckoned with, known to have a wise head on his shoulders. He did not suffer fools gladly and shied away from petty, small-talk-laden social gatherings.

He was hunting wild boar on the Brough family estate, which was in the middle of the United European Landmass. He was riding with two of his army companions, Jeremy, his second-in-command, and Gavin, a close associate who had enrolled at the same time as himself. They both looked ready but nervous. For Hugo, the anticipation, the waiting, was just as thrilling as the chase.

Suddenly below him, at breakneck speed, came a family of wild boar, grunting loudly. On cue, he dug his spurs deep into the flanks of his horse and they were off!

The now squealing wild boar were scattered in front of the posse of riders, threatening to upset them. At the front, Hugo twisted the reins of Firemaker. The spittle from the horse's mouth ran in rivers of white across its neck, which, along with the wild look in its eyes, made it seem possessed.

They were now gaining on the boar.

The light was fading fast, and time was running out. Very soon the riders wouldn't be able to see a thing.

Suddenly, a deafening crack was heard to their right; a flash of lightning, a glow of incandescent light, and Hugo and the other two riders were thrown off their horses, high into the damp woody air.

Hugo hit the ground face first and slid along the forest floor, through the damp detritus of soil, twigs and small stones. He eventually came to a stop and lay there, face down, winded and dazed. He slowly picked himself up and sat upright, spitting a mixture of dirt and blood from his mouth. He turned around to look for the others.

They too were coming around slowly, cursing and groaning.

"What the hell was that?" Hugo groaned.

The mesmerizing bright light to his right caught his eye. The forest around him was bathed in a white, crackling fluorescent light.

He stood up, wiped the mud off his tunic, and slipped the retro gun into his right hand, looking at the white light. The two other riders joined him, mouths open. They too were hypnotically drawn to the phenomenon unfolding before them.

The pulsating light formed a column stretching up from the forest floor through the canopy above them and into the darkening sky, as far as the eye could see. It was approximately ten feet wide, with constantly changing hues, pastel shades of yellow, green, blue and pink.

Hugo picked up a large stick and tentatively threw it at the column. The stick was sucked in and enveloped by the light, disappearing within a fraction of a second.

Silently inching their way towards the column, they felt a slight warmth on their faces and detected a curious smell of ozone that reminded Hugo of the seaside. A constant electrical buzz emanated from it. They stopped near it, transfixed, feeling nauseous. Their hair was standing on end!

Suddenly, a long, slender arm, covered in red material and marked with strange patterns, shot towards them from the column, stopping just short of its shoulder. It seemed to be struggling to penetrate the column. After two or three attempts, the arm retreated into the throbbing, multi-colored light. Shocked, they stumbled back and looked at each other in disbelief, wanting answers.

AN EXTRACT FROM BOOK 2:
KIA THE EMPATH

ᚠᚢᚱᚲ ᚩᚷ ᚱᚦ ᚲᚷᚾᚩ ᚦᚱᚾᚢ ᚱᚾᚩᛁᛁᚲᚦᚱᚷᚦᚱ ᚦᚷ ᚾᚢᚷᚢ ᚷᚾᛁ

*(As one portal closes, another one opens. Accept the new
adventures with open arms. This is how we grow inside)*

Kia was running. She was running as fast as possible. Her
arms were pumping, and she was already out of breath. She
was running through a Melroon forest on the north side of
Salnalyn lake, the home of the water elves, the Pharaas.

She darted this way and that, nearly tripping because she
was running at full pelt. Suddenly, a large black-and-yellow-
striped arrow thudded into a tree trunk inches from her
head. Others followed closely, zipping past her now at an
alarming rate.

She ran blindly through the forest with no thought of
where she was going. Her only thought was to keep out of
the line of sight of the archers. She knew who they were
now. They were the Morg U'Mist. And they were outraged.
These were the assassins of the cosmos. Always up for hire.
No assassination too small. They were a very secretive

species, and had built a reputation over many millennia as a force to be reckoned with. In some ways, they were similar to the ancient Earthan Japanese Ninja warriors. They worked with stealth. With absolute silence. One minute there would be no one there; the next instant you could be surrounded.

Their only drawback was overconfidence. Many times, this had led to failed assassination contracts. They would become lazy because they thought they were unbeatable.

In those early days, when Hugo had arrived through the portal into Laniakeea, there had been an incident when Allana was demonstrating the rules and play of Granthanda, the national bow-and-arrow competition on Laniakeea. Another elf family, envious and jealous of Allana's success, had hired three Morg U'Mist to assassinate Allana. Luckily, the attempt failed. The most the Morg U'Mist were able to do was disable one of Allana's assistants with an arrow that penetrated her left calf. Within a short space of time, Elfistra, with the help of the empaths, found and apprehended the culprits, and discovered which elf family was responsible for setting up the contract. The Morg U'Mist were banished, and the Elf family subjected to the Kralapal ceremony.

On Laniakeea, any form of physical punishment for a misdemeanor had been banned for at least two millennia. It was thought to be more compassionate to introduce the Kralapal. The guilty members would be brought before their own family and close friends, and anyone of the general population that wanted to observe. Then, the family members and friends, in turn, would extol the virtues of the guilty person or family, bringing up all their good points and never any negative aspects. This produced a remarkable effect. The guilty party began to have confidence in themselves and were much more easily able to understand the wrong they had committed.

In most cases the queen would also introduce a material punishment, depending on the severity of the misdemeanor, which could involve banning them from competing in the Granthanda competition, or removing their Barboski for a certain time. But, more than anything, the guilty party knew that more or less everyone on Laniakeea was aware of what they had done, and the embarrassment normally completed the sentence. If an elf or elves had been killed, that was much more serious. Dealing with it was the sole responsibility of the queen.

The evil dark Lord, Rand Raneth, was a case in point. He was a Laniakeean who was banished for killing two elves, and, as we know, had since become leader of a dark magic faction called the Mandaxon, who reside on a dimension tucked away in the west of the cosmos. He constantly tries to attack Laniakeea to steal Elvina the wand.

So Kia was running hell for leather and becoming fearful for her life. She had no idea what she had done to deserve this. She had considered covering herself with a protection spell, which could deflect the majority of the arrows, but you had to be still and concentrate very hard to generate that spell. It was not the easiest spell to construct at the best of times, so she kept on running.

Another arrow passed so close to the top of her head that she felt the feathers at the end of the arrow brush through her hair.

We need to get this in perspective. These arrows were not flimsy children's arrows. They were approximately three feet long. The diameter of the shaft was at least two inches, and the arrowhead itself was cruelly barbed and usually dipped in all manner of incapacitating liquids, that could render you paralyzed, or even, if necessary, a muscle relaxant combined with a poison that would kill you. A most horrible death.

Kia was running out of options when suddenly the trees cleared and she scrabbled hard to stop from falling over a cliff edge that appeared at her feet. She peered over the edge. It was a drop of two hundred feet plus to Salnalyn lake, the home of the water elves, the Pharaas.

Kia breathed a mental sigh of relief. The Laniakeeans were on very good terms with the Pharaas. In fact, many millennia ago, the Pharaas had sought refuge from their own water dimension that was deteriorating through no fault of their own. They searched numerous dimensions and Laniakeea had the perfect lake, Salnalyn.

As with everything else on Laniakeea, the lake was enormous, not just in area (you could quite easily fit all the Earth dimension's seas in the space) but also depth. Again, using a measurement familiar to Earthan's reading this, the depth was equivalent to two and a half Everest's standing end on end, and still the tip would not break the surface of the lake.

Kia had split seconds to decide what to do. The arrows were coming at her relentlessly, so she took a few steps back, ran at the cliff edge and launched herself over the edge.

AN EXTRACT FROM BOOK 3: ETERNITY

ᚾᛁᛜᛁᚾᚢᛞ ᚱᚤᛞ ᚩᛃ ᛀᚱᚱᛞ ᛗᛁᛗᛁᛜ ᚴᛃᚾᛁᛁ ᛗᛃ ᚩᛃ ᚾᛁᛁᛜᚠᛋ ᚦᛃ

(Learn to love yourself, then you will be able to love
those around you)

Rand Raneth was tired. He was hot, very hot, and he vigorously rubbed his eyes. For as far as he could see, there was sand. Sand similar to the sand in the Earthan dimension, but a deeper red or gold. It was also a lot finer than that on Earth, which meant that even the slightest breeze whipped the fine grains into the air, which was why he was rubbing his eyes. The more he rubbed, the more they watered, so he scrabbled for his small bottle of Voovo, uncorked it and poured it into his eyes as quickly as he could. Voovo, the one "cure-all" nearly all Laniakeeans had in their dwellings. It wouldn't just relieve minor medical problems, whether they be human or Elf, but even helped with anxiety and anger problems. (This was restricted to humans, it seemed.) Rand Raneth was a Laniakeean, but had been banished from Laniakeea for murdering two other Laniakeeans. Senseless murder, or even accidental murder, was virtually unheard of on Laniakeea, and the ultimate price was permanent banishment from Laniakeea.

Rand Raneth was grateful for the immediate relief of the itchiness. The blue, slightly effervescing liquid also washed away what grains of Sarzad sand still remained. He wrapped the cloth hanging around his neck around his head. The weave was loose enough to ensure he could see, but only just.

Shortly after he had been banished, Rand Raneth became leader of the easily led Mandaxon, also known as the black arrows, a dark-magic faction. Already he had chalked up four failed attempts to steal Elvina the wand, the last as part of the team working with Jalsaz, the demon, during the battle in the Valley of Storms on Laniakeea. This campaign also failed, but Rand Raneth was determined never to give up until two major problems in his life were resolved. Capturing Elvina the wand, and destroying Queen Haruntha for her decision to banish him to the outer cosmic dimensions. He hated her with a passion. It gnawed away inside him, eating away at his emotions, and created this hateful, hurtful creature which was the antithesis of a normal Laniakeean.

Rand Raneth looked very unusual. He shaved his head and was covered in dark, magical incantation tattoos. He wore only black, monk-like gowns, and often brought his hood over his head so others were not able to see his face.

Rand Raneth was here to meet with just one of the three species of Sarzad that inhabited this dimension. Biologically they all had common traits, although shape and size varied enormously between the three factions. They had one major characteristic in common: they all had a symbiotic relationship with an insect-like creature called the Braal. The Braal was similar in shape to the Earthan trilobites of old. For this symbiotic relationship to exist, every one of the Sarzad species had an indentation on their chests, into which the Braal would fit snugly. The three Sarzad species were the Sass, the Currs and the Sipps.

The Sass were quite small in stature, stocky and extremely hairy; the Currs fairly tall, hairless and very spindly, although joints, such as the knees, ankles, wrists and elbows, were abnormally large and red. The Sipps were different again, being very insect-like, with mandibles, compound eyes, antennae, six pairs of legs. But in each case, apart from the covering on the top surfaces, the size and shape of the Braal, and where they integrated into their host, was almost identical.

From the beginning of their formation, the Sass had always felt they were the superior species in every aspect of Sarzad life. Indeed, they were intellectually far advanced compared to the other two species. However, the Currs and Sips were very resentful of the power the Sass held over them, and for a millennium now there had been squabbles between the Sass, on the one hand, and the Currs and Sipps on the other. It had reached boiling point, murderous boiling point, which was why the Sass had reached out for this very secretive meeting with Rand Raneth.

There was a cosmic information highway, originally perpetrated by the Morg U'Mist, essentially to open up the chance for interested parties who wanted to arrange secretive assassination contracts. But it also provided many other useful information titbits for those species who wanted to pursue other unlawful contracts.

Rand Raneth's band of black arrows were almost as well known as the infamous Morg U'Mist. Their peculiar methods of black magic were feared across all the cosmii. They could create a dark magic series of events that, once initiated, could not be stopped, whether it be directed towards an individual or a whole species. And so it was the Sass that had, to coin a human phase, "put their ear to the railway track," and were able to contact Rand Raneth to meet and "exchange skills acceptable to each species," as the Sass had put it. Rand Raneth researched Sarzad as a dimension, and the historical ranting and raving of the Sass against the Currs and Sipps.

Rand Raneth agreed to a meeting on Sarzad, and he had with him two of his high-ranking Mandaxon warriors, covered from head to toe in black fabric, with their signature black bows and arrows.

As Rand Raneth's vision started to clear, he noticed on the horizon, and approaching at great speed, a huge sandstorm. Deep dark red at the base, with flashes of lightning shooting outwards, and then a wall of sand and clouds rising up into the sky as far as the eye could see.

The two Mandaxon with Rand Raneth were looking nervous, hastily searching every which way for shelter of sorts, but there wasn't any. Rand Raneth frowned. He was at the right coordinates, at the pre-arranged time, and the Sass should have been here. *Fine,* he thought, *I will give them one more cosmic minute, then we are out of here.*

Suddenly, the sand beneath their feet began disappearing, and they found themselves falling head over heels. It took them by surprise, but no sooner were they falling at great speed than they landed, very softly, in a contrasting world underground!

AUTHORS NOTES

Hello and welcome!

First of all, I hope you enjoyed the prequel and extracts from the three books already completed in The Wand Chronicles Trilogy.

I would urge you to join up with the 'Wand Family'. It is absolutely FREE, and I promise your details will be kept very private to the Wand Chronicles.

Simply copy and paste this link into your search engine: https://www.thewand.me/members-1

When you join, I have a special gift for you! (subject to availability) and there will be other free goodies available, including competitions and unusual collectable memorabilia.

I will also personally welcome any new addition to the 'Wand family'

All the books, in either paperback and kindle, may be found on Amazon. Simply search for:

The Wand Chronicles: Elfistra the Sorceress

The Wand Chronicles: Kia the Empath

The Wand Chronicles: Eternity

If you know of anyone who would like a FREE copy of this prequel, either in paperback or as an Ebook, please suggest they look on Amazon or email me at: thewandchronicles@gmail.com

To an Author, reviews are so very important, so I would please request you write a few sentences on Amazon. Thank you.

An extra addition I include in all three books is a quick and easy reference glossary, so you can keep up-to-date with the characters, who they are and where they are from, plus a section dedicated to the correct phonetic pronunciation of some of the more complex names and places.

I am very interested in people, just as I am in the characters I create, both human and elf and otherwise, that crop up in my adventures, so please, do email me with any thoughts and questions, and I promise to reply to every email received.

With your help, The Wand Chronicles will be a huge success!

Thank you

Michael Ross
New Mills, High Peak, Derbyshire, UK

Elvina the Wand.

(The most powerful wand in the cosmos)

The Krandokrall, the keepers of Spiritwood on Laniakeea
whose sole purpose is to protect the Sola Tree containing
Elvina the Wand

Jalsaz, the magical demon. One of many beings that tries
to steal Elvina the Wand.

Morg Spear'Nd, spiritual leader of the Morg U'Mist
The most feared assassins in the whole of the cosmos

The Wand Chronicles – The Prequel

46451161R00038

Printed in Poland
by Amazon Fulfillment
Poland Sp. z o.o., Wrocław